Uncle Nehru,

Please send An Elephant!

Tulika

Uncle Nehru, Please Send An Elephant!

Text DEVIKA CARIAPA

Pictures SATWIK GADE

One afternoon, when Prime Minister Nehru opened his overstuffed mail bag, he was in for a surprise — out tumbled more than a thousand colourfully decorated cards and letters! They came from the children of the Taito Ward of Tokyo, Japan.

Jawaharlal Nehru always loved to hear what children had to say. So, even though he had lots to do, he sat down to read.

"Sorry to disturb you, Prime Minister," the letters said, *"we know you're a busy person. But we have never seen a live elephant. Could you kindly send us one from India? We promise to look after it very carefully."*

Prime Minister Nehru was certainly a very busy person. He had a newly independent country to run. A country that needed food and houses, electricity, roads and factories.

But he knew that Japan had problems too. A terrible world war had just ended. Like many other countries, it was in ruins and the people were having a very hard time.

Although India and Japan had been enemies during the war, Prime Minister Nehru felt that India should now work as friends with other nations so that there would be peace in the future.

So, he called his aides and said, "Let's send an elephant to the children of Japan!"

First, they had to find the right elephant. In the forests near Mysore they found a great beauty, with a broad forehead and a long trunk. And not just that — everyone said she was special. Because while most Asian elephants have eighteen toenails, she had sixteen — four on each foot!

Prime Minister Nehru named her Indira, after his daughter. No one knows what his daughter Indira thought of having an elephant named after her!

Indira the elephant left on the freighter ship *Encho Maru* from Calcutta in August 1949. The voyage was long and rough, and she was seasick all the way. When she finally arrived at Yokohama port about a month later, excited crowds had gathered on the quay to greet her. Among them were many of those letter writers from the Taito Ward.

But Indira threw a huge tantrum and refused to get off the ship! For two days, everyone watched in dismay as she sidestepped and dodged her handlers.

When she finally decided to get off, she stepped out like a queen. Amidst cheers and banners saying 'Welcome Miss Indira', she calmly walked through the streets to Tokyo Zoo!

Prime Minister Nehru had sent a letter with Indira. It said:

> "I hope that when the children of India and the children of Japan will grow up, they will serve not only their great countries but also the cause of peace and cooperation all over Asia and the World. So you must look upon this elephant ... as a messenger of affection and goodwill from the children of India. The elephant is a noble animal. It is wise and patient, strong, and yet, gentle. I hope all of us will also develop these qualities."

Indira was now India's ambassador of peace, and a symbol of friendship between the Japanese and Indian people.

A few years later, a little boy named Peter Marmorek in the town of Granby, Canada, listened carefully as his father read out a report from the newspaper. It said that the mayor of their little town had travelled to India and asked Prime Minister Nehru if he could send an elephant for Granby Zoo. The prime minister had replied:

> "If the children of Granby want an elephant, I will try and dig one up."

IF?! Of course the children of Granby wanted an elephant! Peter sprang into action. Since he was only five years old and couldn't spell very well as yet, he dictated a letter for his father to type.

Dear Prime Minister Nehru,

The children of Granby would be very happy to have an elephant from India. Kindly send us one as soon as possible. Thank you for your kind offer.

P.S. I didn't know elephants lived underground and hope it's not too much of a problem to dig one up.

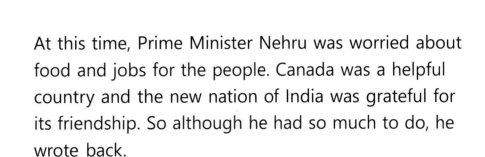

At this time, Prime Minister Nehru was worried about food and jobs for the people. Canada was a helpful country and the new nation of India was grateful for its friendship. So although he had so much to do, he wrote back.

Two weeks later, Peter received an official looking letter from India sealed with a red wax stamp.

Prime Minister Nehru wrote:

"Dear Peter,

Elephants do not live underground. They are very big animals and they wander about in the forests ... It is not easy to catch them."

But, he assured Peter, he would be delighted to find one for Granby.

Everyone in Canada was very excited that Peter had a personal reply from the prime minister of India. He became quite a celebrity, with requests for interviews and his photographs in the newspapers.

Prime Minister Nehru kept his promise. A clever three-year-old elephant from Kerala named Ambika was found and trained, even getting English lessons from a special teacher so that she could communicate with the Canadians.

Two years later, Ambika lumbered into Granby Zoo. Peter was part of the welcome committee. He had prepared a speech. But when he saw Ambika, he became a little nervous. She was so much bigger than he had imagined!

"Don't worry," his father said, "elephants are vegetarian."

Peter looked uncertain. "But how does she know I'm not a vegetable?!"

Many years later, a grown-up Peter said he had learned from Ambika "that India was a magical country — if you wrote to it, they would send you an elephant."

By now, Prime Minister Nehru was getting used to children asking him for elephants. So he wasn't surprised when he received a rather wobbly handwritten letter from an eight-year-old in the Netherlands named Thea de Boer.

> Dear Mister Nehru,
>
> I should like so very much to see an elephant...
> Is it not possible for you to arrange this?

Attached to her letter was a note addressed to "Uncle Nehru". It was signed by thousands of Dutch schoolchildren who, like Thea, also wanted more than anything to see an elephant.

The prime minister, now hard at work setting up schools
and scientific institutes, thought it an excellent idea to show
India's friendly nature to people all over the world.

So, Murugan was sent for the children of the Netherlands. He was greeted like a superstar at Amsterdam Zoo, with crowds of cheering schoolchildren waving homemade Indian flags. His photographs were splashed all over the newspapers and magazines.

Soon India's elephants were travelling all over the world by ship and train and road.

In those days, no one thought of asking the elephants how they felt about travelling to distant countries. Maybe some of them saw it as a grand adventure. Others may have been miserable without their friends and their warm, familiar jungles. Clever scientists have now learnt that elephants are sensitive creatures with deep attachments to their families.

If Prime Minister Nehru had known this, he would not have sent elephants so far from home!

But those were different times. And children everywhere waited eagerly to welcome their special jumbo friends from India.

Thirteen-year-old Asha from Assam went all the way to China. First she travelled by steamer ship to Hong Kong. She then transferred to a special railway wagon that chugged across to Beijing.

On the 21-day journey, she was sick once. But she still managed to eat her way through 725 kilos of bread and leaves, 363 kilos of hay and straw, 1000 bananas, 80 sticks of sugarcane and 18 kilos of salt!

When she arrived in Beijing, she politely curtseyed on one knee before Chou En-Lai, the head of the Chinese government, and presented a message from Prime Minister Nehru for the children of China.

Meanwhile in Turkey, a children's magazine organised a drawing competition, in which readers were asked to send in their very best cartoon of an elephant. Not many Turkish children had seen a real elephant. But the magazine's office was flooded with thousands of cards, letters and scraps of paper with drawings of elephants on them. The magazine decided to publish an open letter to Prime Minister Nehru.

Could the children of Turkey please have a REAL elephant?

Mohini the two-year-old elephant was India's gift to the children of Turkey. When she arrived in Istanbul, she was received like a celebrity! The cover page of the magazine was a cartoon of Mohini's welcome ceremony.

And soon after, Ravi and Shashi went together to Soviet Russia, and Ambika the Second to the United States of America.

Prime Minster Nehru's elephant ambassadors made children all over the world smile. Everyone saw that the new country of India, although so far away and so busy with problems of its own, could take the time to be generous. India was seen as a gentle, noble friend who answered your letters and sent GINORMOUS presents!

For B S Chengapa.
Legendary forester and my beloved grandfather — Devika

Uncle Nehru, Please Send An Elephant! (English)

ISBN 978-81-949817-7-0
© *text* Devika Cariapa
© *illustrations* Satwik Gade
First published in India, 2021

Published by
Tulika Publishers, 305 Manickam Avenue, TTK Road, Alwarpet, Chennai 600 018, India
email reachus@tulikabooks.com *website* www.tulikabooks.com

Printed by
Sudarsan Graphics, Chennai, India